# The Only
# Rosie Ma

Written and illustrated
by Charlotte Middleton

**Collins**

Gnawdon Woods is a very picturesque place and home to a family of mice. They live in a house that's so tiny it's almost invisible!

Inside the house, Rosie squeaked, "I know that I look like my family ... but I'd prefer to resemble the other mice at school."

“What’s wrong with
our wonderfully
wobbly whiskers?”
asked Dad.

“And our wonderfully
wavy fur?” questioned
Joey, combing it
into place.

“And our long
gnashing teeth –
perfect for gnawing!”
Mum said.

Rosie was emotional. “But we also have knobbly knees and little limbs!”

“I really don’t want to be the only Rosie Maloney,” she said passionately.

At school Rosie climbed onto the bench to place her coat on the hook.

"Everybody is taller than me," she complained to Constance.

In class, she wrinkled her nose. “Nobody has wavy fur like me. It would be nice to have smooth fur!”

Rosie studied Lola’s face. “It would be magnificent to have neat whiskers!” she said.

While gnawing a crumbly nut, she said to Christopher,
"It would be nice to have short sturdy teeth!"

"And little limbs are useless in a hurdles race!" exclaimed Rosie.

At the house, Rosie found a lotion labelled "Extra-strong hold for whiskers".

"I can turn my wobbly whiskers into neat rows," said Rosie. She measured out the icy cold liquid and dipped her whiskers in.

With a steady motion she combed them carefully.

Rosie found some wool and instructions: "How to knit a wrap".

"I can conceal my wavy fur and knobbly knees!"

Next she found a bit of wood. She gnawed it into large soles, then she put in place sturdy springs.

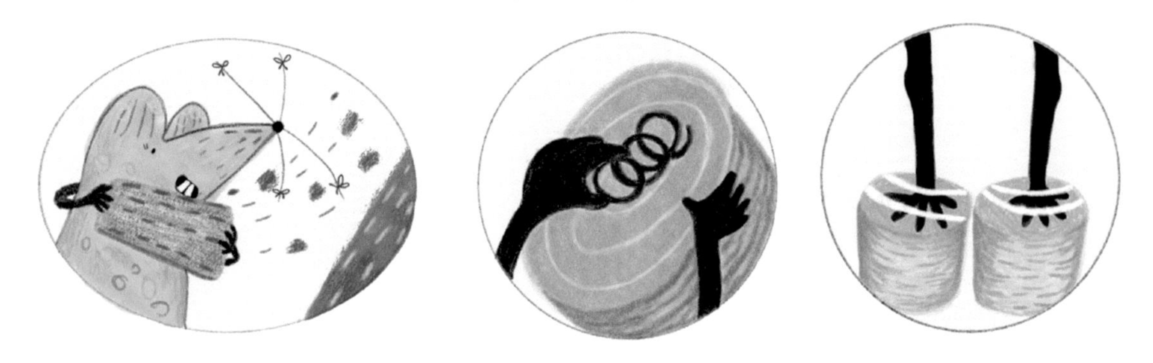

Now Rosie had longer limbs, stumpy teeth and springy feet!

At school, Rosie didn't have to climb to hang her coat up!

But it was challenging in class. There wasn't space for Rosie's legs under the table.

In singing practice, Rosie was pleased – she looked like the other mice!

But her friends couldn't find her and she was so hot in her wrap she sang the wrong notes …

Lola's face was full of sadness when they combed their whiskers.

At lunch time, Rosie took so long to gnaw the nuts with her stubby teeth that there wasn't a chance to play.

At the hurdles race, Rosie's springs were too springy!

Rosie was pink and gasping from the exercise. She made a decision. "I don't want to resemble the other mice any more!"

Rosie threw off her knitted wrap and combed her wonderfully wavy fur.

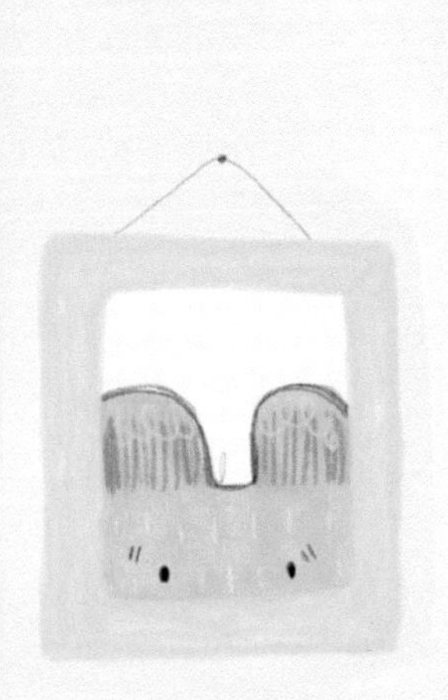

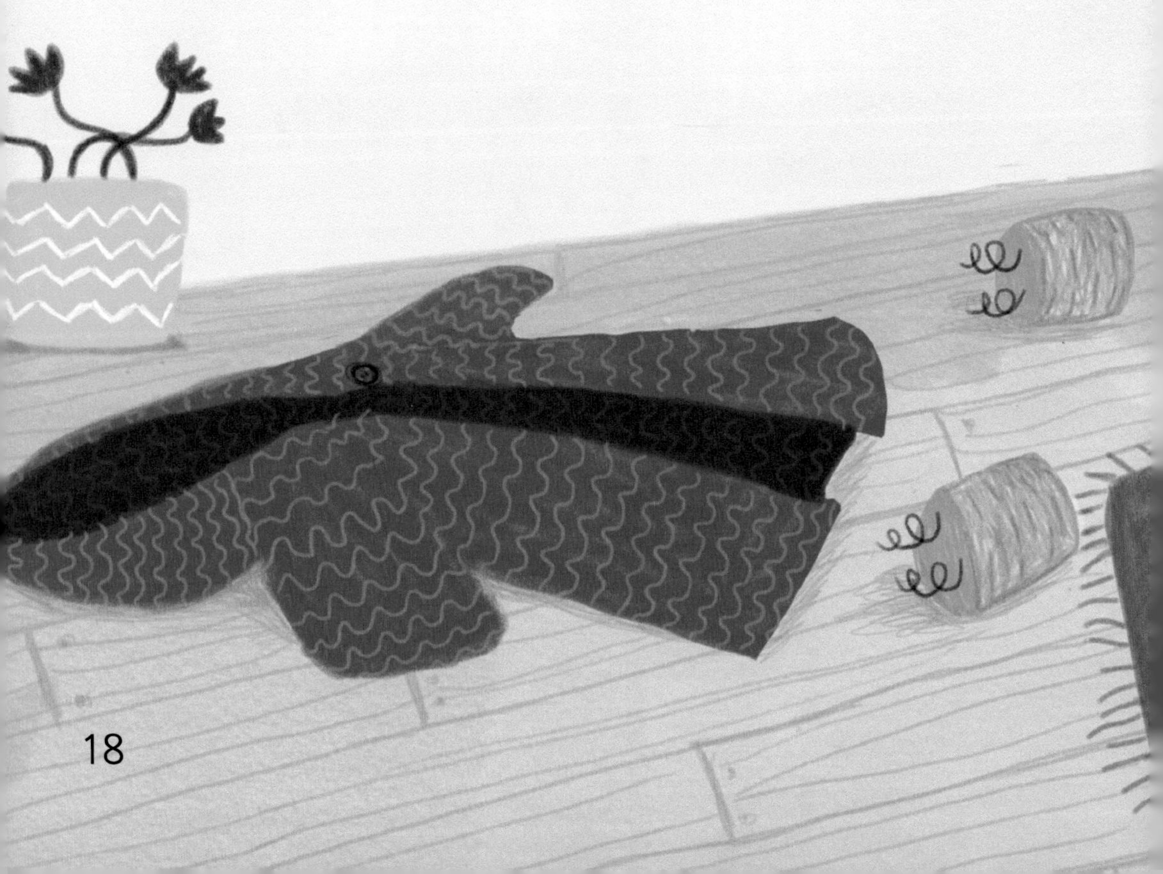

She washed off the lotion – her whiskers were wobbly again.

When she smiled in the mirror, she noticed that her teeth were already growing longer.

"It's much nicer being me!" Rosie cried emotionally. "Everybody is different!"

"I may have knobbly knees and come last at the races at school," said Rosie to her family, "but it's perfectly magnificent to be the one and only Rosie Maloney!"

# After reading

**Letters and Sounds:** Phases 5–6

**Word count:** 495

**Focus phonemes:** /c/ que, x /sh/ ssi, ti, si /zh/ s /m/ mb /n/ kn, gn /s/ c, ce /r/ wr

**Common exception words:** of, to, the, so, our, into, are, said, beautiful, friends, their, were, any, one

**Curriculum links:** Science; PSHE

**National Curriculum learning objectives:** Reading/word reading: apply phonic knowledge and skills as the route to decode words, read common exception words, noting unusual correspondences between spelling and sound and where these occur in the word; Reading/comprehension: develop pleasure in reading, motivation to read, vocabulary and understanding by being encouraged to link what they read or hear to their own experiences

## Developing fluency

- Your child may enjoy hearing you read the book.
- One of you could take the part of Rosie and the other all the other characters. Take turns to be the narrator. Model reading the speech with expression.

## Phonic practice

- Talk about how the same sound can be written in different ways. For example, the /sh/ sound is spelled differently in each of the following words:

  mission      emotional      decision
- Ask your child to sound talk and blend each of the words.
- Talk about the different ways the /sh/ sound is spelled in these words. (*ssi, ti, si*)
- Can your child think of any other words that contain the /sh/ sound? How is /sh/ spelled in those words?

## Extending vocabulary

- There are some very interesting words in this story. Turn to page 2. Point out the word, **picturesque**. Ask your child:
  - Do you know what this means? (*looks very appealing*)
  - Can you think of another word that the author could have used instead of picturesque? (*pretty, beautiful*)
- Now look at another page in the book. Can your child find an interesting word? Ask them the questions above and discuss the author's choice of words together.